The Adventures of A

MW00882799

"A Day At The Zoo"

By: Christopher Trotter

Dedication

This book is dedicated to all the curious

and adventurous children who find joy in the world's wonders.

Christian, at 5 years old, is experiencing all the experiences

of learning what life is like, and here,

I documented those experiences through his eyes

to allow other children and readers of all ages to see his perspective.

To my wife, Thank You for bringing such a wonderful soul

into our lives and inspiring me to put Pen to Paper.

Copyright

Copyright © 2024 Christopher Trotter

All rights reserved.

No part of this book may be reproduced, distributed,

or transmitted in any form or by any means,

without the prior written permission of the author,

except in the case of brief quotations embodied in critical reviews

and certain other noncommercial uses permitted by copyright law.

Published by Christopher Trotter

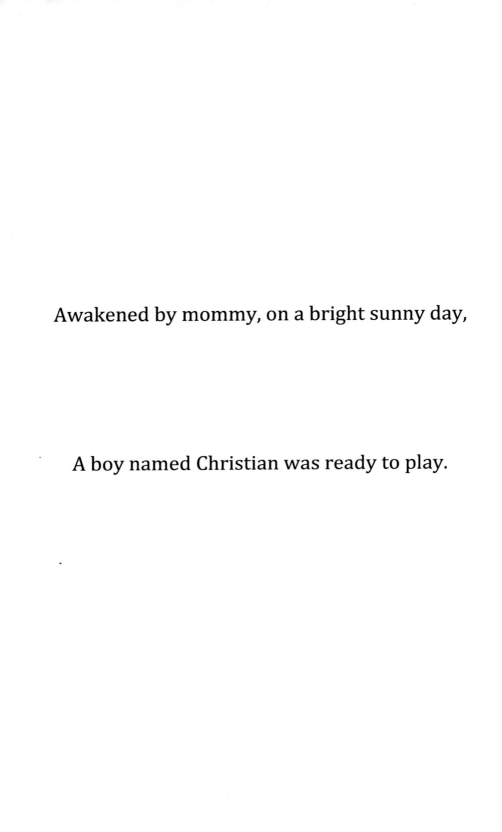

Awakened by mommy, on a bright sunny day,

A boy named Christian was ready to play.

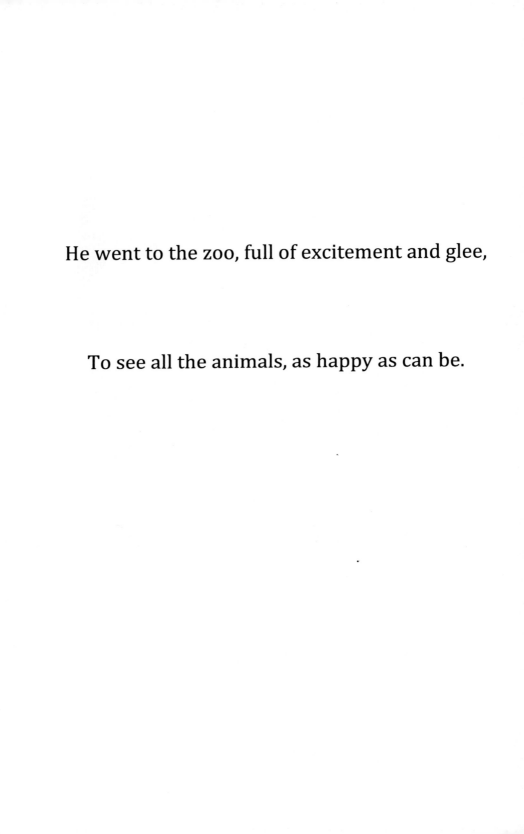

He went to the zoo, full of excitement and glee,

To see all the animals, as happy as can be.

Christian jogged down the pathway,

Looking both left and right.

With the smell of the jungle, and

The wild in his sights.

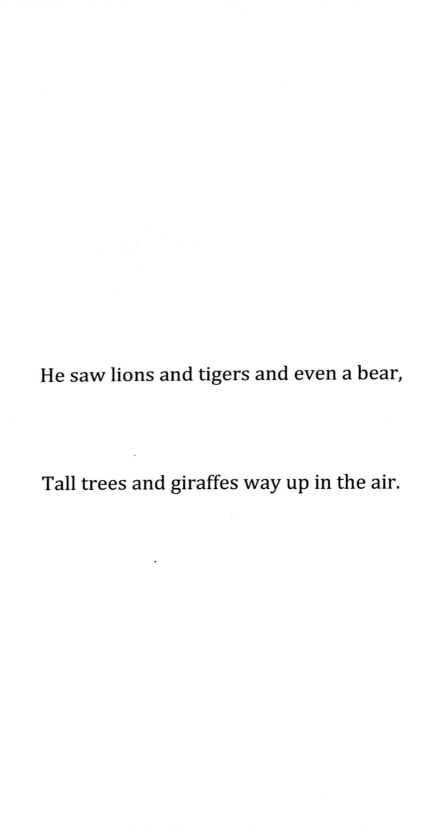

He saw lions and tigers and even a bear,

Tall trees and giraffes way up in the air.

Next, Christian stared at the lions, so strong and grand,

Sitting on top of a mound, tail wagging the sand.

With their manes all flowing, they looked so serene,

Christian sat and watched, in awe of this scene.

As he and mommy walked along, on this special day,

He saw a panda sleeping, in a bamboo sway.

Its black and white fur looked so soft as can be,

Christian smiled and wished he could cuddle it, to see.

Lastly, Christian came to the elephant's place,

Its trunk swinging freely, with grace and pace.

Christian fed it some fruit, and it ate it so fast,

This was an experience he wanted to last.

But then, Mommy said

"Christian it's time to end our day at the zoo,"

Christian felt sad but knew what to do.

"We'll be back soon, for another great day,

With all the animals who love to play!"

The End

Made in United States
Orlando, FL
03 January 2025

56686273R00018